Usborne Forgotten Fairy Tales

Clever Molly

Retold by Rosie Dickins

Illustrated by Alessandra Santelli

Reading consultant: Alison Kelly

About
Forgotten Fairy Tales

People have been telling each other fairy tales for thousands of years. Then, a few hundred years ago, collectors began writing the stories down. The ones that became famous were the ones that reflected the ideas of the time.

These stories had patient, polite princesses such as *Snow White* and *Sleeping Beauty*. The tales with bold girls fighting their own battles were ignored.

This series brings to life the stories of those forgotten brave and brilliant girls...

Contents

Chapter 1   5
A house in the forest

Chapter 2   10
The giant

Chapter 3   18
The king's challenge

Chapter 4   25
Molly goes back

Chapter 5   34
A sack and a stick

About the story   46

Chapter 1

A house in the forest

Molly and her sisters stared at their empty plates. Their tummies rumbled loudly.

"What shall we do?" said one
of the sisters.

"Why, go and find food," said
Molly. So off they went.

At last, they came to a forest.
A huge stone house stood among
the trees.

"It must belong to a giant," said the other sister nervously.

"Then I'll ask for something GIANT to eat," said Molly.

Molly knocked. *Rat-a-tat-tat!*

A woman peeked out. "What do you want?" she said. "My husband is a giant. If he finds you, he'll gobble you up!"

"Please, we're SO hungry," begged Molly. "Can you spare any food?"

The woman hesitated. Then she nodded. "All right, come in. Hurry! You must go before he gets back."

Chapter 2

The giant

Inside, three girls were eating bowls of bread and milk. They were the giant's daughters.

The woman filled three more bowls. Molly and her sisters had barely lifted their spoons when they heard footsteps...

Thump

Thump

Thump

BANG!

The door crashed open.
The giant was home early.

"Now, dear," said his wife.
"It's just three girls I invited in."
"We must be going," added
Molly quickly.

"No," said the giant, shutting the door. "It's far too late. You must stay the night. You can sleep beside my daughters."

At bedtime, the giant gave each of his daughters a chain of gold. For Molly and her sisters, he took wisps of straw and made them each a chain of straw.

Molly didn't trust the giant.
When the other girls fell asleep,
she switched the chains so she
and her sisters were wearing the
gold ones. Then she waited.

Sometime later, the giant came and reached out... If he felt a straw chain, he seized that girl and stuffed her into a sack. If he felt gold, he left her alone.

"That'll be a tasty breakfast!" he chuckled, going back to bed.

Soon, giant snores filled the air. Molly let out a deep breath and nudged her sisters.

"Time to go!"

Chapter 3

The king's challenge

Molly and her sisters tiptoed outside. Then they ran, until they came to a clifftop.

Far below, a river tumbled over jagged rocks. In front of them stretched a single rope. "It's like a bridge made of one hair," said Molly.

The sisters were afraid to cross, so Molly ran lightly over to show them how.

They walked on and on. After a while they came to a castle which belonged to a king.

"How did you get here?" the king asked the sisters.

"Through the forest and over the bridge of one hair."

The king stared. "Didn't you meet the wicked giant?"

"Oh yes," said
Molly. "He tried to
eat us, but we escaped."
   The king nodded slowly.
"I have offered half my kingdom
to anyone who defeats that
giant," he said. "Will you try?"

22

"How?" asked Molly.

"The giant has three treasures which give him his strength," the king told her.

A shield of iron...

a purse full of silver...

...and a ring of gold.

"You'd have to steal them."

"All right," agreed Molly. "I like a challenge." Her tummy rumbled. "But I'll need a good breakfast first!"

Chapter 4

Molly goes back

At nightfall, Molly crept back to the giant's house. Through the window, she saw the shield hanging on the wall.

She waited until the giant, his wife and daughters were all snoring. Then she tiptoed inside and reached up...

Clitter!
Clatter!

The shield rattled and the giant sprang awake.

Quick as a flash, Molly
grabbed the shield and ran.
She ran back to the bridge
of one hair and across it, and
the giant could not follow.

"You'll be sorry, girl," he
yelled, shaking a giant fist.
"Never come this way again!"
"I'll be back twice more,"
she replied, laughing.

The next night, Molly came for the purse. She saw the giant tuck it under his pillow before he went to sleep.

Once he was snoring, she tiptoed in and reached out...

The coins inside shifted and the giant sprang awake.

Molly was already running away with the purse.

Quick as a flash, Molly ran to the bridge and across it.

"You'll be sorry, girl," the giant yelled after her. "Never come this way again!"

"I'll be back once more," she replied, laughing.

On the third night Molly
came for the ring, which the
giant wore on his thumb.

This time, the giant snored louder than ever. But perhaps he was only pretending. As Molly pulled off the ring, he pounced... "GOTCHA!"

Chapter 5

A sack and a stick

"I've got you, you pesky thief!" crowed the giant. "Now, what shall I do with you?"

Molly had an answer ready. "If I were you, I'd tie me in a sack so I couldn't run away. Then, I'd go outside and find a stick to beat me."

"Very well," said the
giant, with a nasty chuckle.
He dropped Molly into a sack,
tied it tightly and went out
to find a stick.

As soon as the giant had left,
Molly began to sing loudly.

"What CAN you see?" asked
the giant's wife, coming in.

Molly didn't reply, but kept on singing.

If you could see what I see...

The giant's wife itched with curiosity. She opened the sack and took Molly's place, so she could see for herself.

Molly was free! Quick as a flash, she was up and running – taking the ring with her.

Thump

Thump

Thump

Heavy footsteps shook the floor. The giant was back.

He lifted his stick, ready for a good thwack... when his wife popped her head out.

"I see nothing but sackcloth!" she yelled.

"W-what?" The giant dropped the stick. "Where's the girl?"

He glanced out of
the window – and saw
Molly disappearing.
With a roar of rage,
he raced after her.

The giant ran, and Molly ran.
When they came to the bridge,
Molly ran over but the giant
had to stop.

"You'll be sorry, girl," he
yelled furiously. "NEVER
come this way again!"

"Don't worry, I won't," said Molly, grinning. "Not now I have this." She held up the ring, glinting in the sunlight.

The giant roared once more...
but all that came out was a
squeak. His power was gone. He
never troubled anyone again.

The king was delighted. True to his word, he gave Molly half his kingdom – and she and her sisters lived happily ever after.

About the story

This story of a bold, clever girl saving herself and her sisters is a traditional Scottish tale. A similar tale is told in Ireland.

The retelling in this book is based on versions published over a hundred years ago, by Joseph Jacobs and Flora Annie Steel.

Both those writers
gave Molly's full name
as Molly Whuppie.
In Scotland, 'whuppie' or
'whippy' can mean 'nimble'
or 'clever'.

Designed by Laura Bridges
Series designer: Russell Punter
Series editor: Lesley Sims

First published in 2020 by Usborne Publishing Ltd.,
Usborne House. 83-85 Saffron Hill, London EC1N 8RT, England.
usborne.com

48